MIKE MAIHACK

CLEOPATRA
IN SPACE

BOOK FIVE
FALLEN EMPIRES

graphix

AN IMPRINT OF

◣SCHOLASTIC

Library of Congress Control Number: 2017962946

ISBN 978-1-338-20413-1 (hardcover)
ISBN 978-1-338-20412-4 (paperback)

10 9 8 7 6 5 4 3 2 1   19 20 21 22 23

Printed in China   38
First edition, April 2019
Edited by Cassandra Pelham Fulton
Book design by Phil Falco
Creative Director: David Saylor

J-GN
CLEOPATRA IN SPACE
466-4184

CHAPTER ONE

FLASH

CRACK

GET UP.

SPLASH

GET UP!

I HOPE YOU CAN MAINTAIN THAT WIT WHEN YOU GREET ANUBIS NEXT WEEK, OLD MAN.

GIVE BLESSINGS TO THE GODS THAT SNIVELING ROMAN, OCTAVIANUS, HAS BEEN KEEPING THE PHARAOH SO OCCUPIED THIS YEAR OR HE PROBABLY WOULD HAVE ORDERED YOUR DEATHS MONTHS AGO.

YES, HOW FORTUNATE FOR US THAT WE'VE BEEN GRANTED THE PLEASURE OF YOUR POLITE COMPANY INSTEAD. I THANK THE GODS EVERY DAY.

WELL DONE.

YOU JUST WON YOURSELF ANOTHER DAY WITHOUT FOOD.

GOOD FORTUNE CONTINUES TO SHINE UPON US!

TWO DAYS!

YOU ONLY AGITATE THEM, BAKARI.

MAYBE IF YOU WERE LESS COMPLACENT, WE'D AT LEAST HAVE GOTTEN FRESH BREAD IN HERE THESE PAST TWO YEARS.

CRACK

GET
UP!

GOZI,
GET UP!

BAKARI...?

SOMETHING'S
HAPPENED.

HUMMMMMM...

HUMMMMMMM...

HUMMM MMMMMMM MMM

OOh

OOWAO

CAREFUL. DON'T MOVE.

I'VE BANDAGED WHAT I COULD.

WHAT...?

WHERE...?

WITH THE GODS. I'M NOT SURE WHAT THE PHARAOH COULD HAVE DONE TO ANGER THEM SO, BUT THEIR VENGEANCE WAS SWIFT.

THE PALACE, PERHAPS ALL OF EGYPT... GONE.

GONE...?

I WAS ABLE TO GET US TO ONE OF THEIR BOATS. OFFERED THEM OUR SERVICES. THEY MUST HAVE FELT PITY FOR US. ALLOWED US TO STAY.

WE ARE WITH OUR ANCESTORS NOW.

WHERE IS THAT CABIN BOY?!

CAPTAIN.

THERE'S A SPOT ON THE DECK.

ABOUT TIME, YOU WRETCHED THING.

DRIP

I'LL CLEAN IT UP RIGHT AWAY.

OF COURSE YOU WILL. AND TELL YOUR CABIN-MATE TO BE FASTER ABOUT CATALOGING MY PLUNDER. WE REACH HYKOSIS IN TWO DAYS.

CREEK

CAPTAIN GRU'AT SAID WE REACH PORT IN A COUPLE DAYS.

CREEK

MM HM, YES, YES.

I AM STILL COMPLETELY FASCINATED BY THESE TABLETS. I'M STARTING TO BELIEVE THEY MAY NOT HAVE BEEN CARVED BY MAN AT ALL.

I TOLD YOU TO PUT THOSE AWAY, BAKARI.

THEY'RE EVIL.

THEY...

TOOK HER.

MADE ME THIS WAY.

YOUR SKIN. IT STILL BURNS, DOESN'T IT?

ALL THE TIME.

ARE YOU FINALLY READY TO SERVE ME, GOZI?

GOZI?

GOZI DIED A LONG, LONG TIME AGO.

OCTAVIAN.

GET UP.

EVERYTHING OKAY?

YES, YES. JUST AN OVERLOADED BREAKER.

I GOT IT.

HEY, BRIAN.

OR DO I SAY *ENSIGN* BRIAN, NOW?

IT WOULD BE ENSIGN *BELL*, CLEO. AND JUST BRIAN IS FINE.

SHOULDN'T YOU BE IN COMBAT CLASS?

NOT FOR A FEW MINUTES. WORKING OUT BEFORE.

DON'T YOU EVER GET TIRED?

NOT REALLY.

HMM...

HOW'S THE SHIELD WORK GOING?

JUST CALIBRATING A FEW MINOR THINGS. WE SHOULD STILL BE READY FOR THE LAUNCH TOMORROW NIGHT.

fizz Sprik

I NEVER THOUGHT I'D BE EXCITED ABOUT THE DISRUPTION OF TECHNOLOGY, BUT IF THIS WORKS, IT'S GOING TO HELP A LOT OF PLANETS.

IF NO WEAPONS OR SHIPS CAN BREAK THROUGH THE ATMOSPHERE...

NO XERX CAN THREATEN THE GALAXY.

AND WITH STILL NO SIGN OF OCTAVIAN, YOU MIGHT FINALLY BE ABLE TO RETURN TO YOUR OWN TIME, CLEOPATRA.

YEAH...

MAKING SURE THE SHIELD FUNCTIONS PROPERLY IS MAINLY JUST A MATTER OF BALANCING THE CORRECT FREQUENCIES BETWEEN CADA'DUUN'S AND OUR TECHNOLOGY. SOMETIMES THEY DON'T GET ALONG.

FWOOSH!

FWIIISSH

WE ARE OPTIMISTIC.

RIGHT.

LAST... TIME... I... LISTEN... TO... YOU.

TOMORROW... SPENDING... ALL... DAY... IN... LIBRARY.

Y'KNOW. I JUST REALIZED I HAVE VERY BORING FRIENDS.

HEY!

BOOKS ARE IMPORTANT, CLEO. IN CASE YOU FORGOT, THE ALEXANDRIA LIBRARY HOLDS ALMOST NINETY PERCENT OF THE LAST WRITTEN TEXTS IN THE NILE GALAX--

YEAH, YEAH, YEAH. I KNOW.

YAY BOOKS.

YAY ELECTRONICS AND STUFF.

I'M GOING TO GO BEAT UP SOME FELLOW CADETS FOR TRAINING PURPOSES.

C'MON, AKILA!

HEY, AKILA...

IF YOU DON'T MIND, LET CLEO KNOW I'D LIKE TO RUN ANOTHER TEST ON HER PHYSIOLOGY.

REALLY? SHE JUST RAN, LIKE, TWENTY MILES WITHOUT WORKING UP A SWEAT.

THAT'S KIND OF THE REASON WHY. JUST LET HER KNOW, OKAY?

HOW'S THE NEW ARM HOLDING UP?

BARELY EVEN FEEL IT.

HONESTLY, I THINK I'M BEGINNING TO LIKE IT EVEN MORE THAN I DID MY REAL ARM.

AND NOW BEING ABLE TO HOLD YOUR OWN AGAINST CLEO DURING TARGET PRACTICE PROBABLY HAS NOTHING TO DO WITH THAT, I'M SURE.

MAYBE A LITTLE.

THANKS AGAIN, BRIAN.

SMACK!

GOOD LUCK WITH YOUR ELECTRONICS AND STUFF!

YOU'RE LETTING HER RUN OFF AGAIN.

QUIET, TALIBATH.

VRAK VRAK VRAK VRAK VRAK VRAK VRAK VRAK

I FEEL *FINE*, AKILA.

OW.

VRAK

DON'T HURT THE MESSENGER, CLEO. TAKE IT UP WITH BRIAN.

SORRY. IT'S JUST... I MEAN, I HARDLY EVEN *GLOW* THESE DAYS.

YOU'RE GLOWING RIGHT NOW.

HARDLY.

I SAID HARDLY.

NOTING TO SEE, BYRON.

swish

♪

swish

TAKE A BREATHER, CLASS!

WE HAVE SOME SPECIAL GUESTS WITH US TODAY.

EVERYONE, PLEASE ADDRESS YOUR ATTENTION.

WHOA.

WHAT IS PHARAOH YOSIRA DOING HERE?

GREETINGS, CADETS. PROFESSOR PTOLMINIC HAS INFORMED ME THAT THIS IS HIS MOST ELITE COMBAT TRAINING CLASS. WATCHING YOU TRAIN FOR THE PAST HALF HOUR, I FEEL WITH ALL CONFIDENCE THAT WE CAN CONCUR WITH THAT ASSESSMENT.

WOULDN'T YOU AGREE, YOUR MAJESTY?

Nod

AS YOU ARE ALL AWARE, TOMORROW WE CELEBRATE THE LAUNCH OF OUR NEW PLANETARY SHIELD SYSTEM. IF SUCCESSFUL, IT'LL NOT ONLY AID A GREAT MANY PLANETS IN OUR OWN AILUROS SYSTEM, BUT COUNTLESS CITIES AND COMMUNITIES IN OTHER SYSTEMS OF THE NILE GALAXY AS WELL.

ONE SUCH CITY IS THE REASON WE HAVE THE TECHNOLOGY TO BUILD THE SHIELD IN THE FIRST PLACE, AND THIS MORNING WE RECEIVED SOME IMAGES INFORMING US THAT THEY COULD BE THE TARGET OF AN ATTACK.

SHE'S TALKING ABOUT CADA'DUUN.

AKILA, YOUR PARENTS ARE ON CADA'DUUN.

UH, CLEO...

YOU'RE GLOWING EVEN MORE NOW.

HUH?

NOW, WITH OCTAVIAN PRESUMED DEAD, THERE'S LITTLE REASON TO BELIEVE THE XERX WOULD THREATEN CADA'DUUN ON THEIR OWN. STILL, A LONE XERX VESSEL WAS SPOTTED NEAR THE ELTORIAN SYSTEM. LIKELY A STRAGGLER, BUT AS A PRECAUTIONARY MEASURE, WE WILL BE SELECTING A FEW CADETS TO HELP AID THE P.Y.R.A.M.I.D. OFFICERS STATIONED NEAR THE CITY IN THE OFF-CHANCE AN ATTACK IS IMMINENT.

UGGGHH...

CLEO?

THIS WOULD OF COURSE MEAN MISSING TOMORROW'S SHIELD CELEBRATION--

EHHHH...

BUT YOU WOULD BE PROTECTING A VERY SPECIAL SUBSTANCE THAT...

CADET CLEOPATRA...

ARE YOU ALL RIGHT?

Ooh.

MEDICAL!

INJURED CADET IN COMBAT TRAINING ROOM FOUR!

...

DO YOU REMEMBER WHAT HAPPENED?

YEAH, I FELT A PAIN AND...

BYRON!

IS BYRON ALL RIGHT?

I DIDN'T...

RELAX. CADET BRAMBLES WOKE UP A FEW HOURS AGO.

HE'S A LITTLE BRUISED BUT THE DOCTORS SAY HE'LL BE ABLE TO WALK OUT OF HERE IN THE MORNING.

BYRON'S A LOT TOUGHER THAN YOU GIVE HIM CREDIT FOR, CLEO.

HOLD STILL.

HAVE YOU BEEN GLOWING A LOT LATELY?

MORE THAN USUAL, I MEAN.

NO.

BEEP BEEP BEEP

I WAS JUST TELLING AKILA, HARDLY AT ALL.

HMM...

STOP DOING THAT.

SERIOUSLY, BRIAN. JUST TELL US WHAT YOU'RE THINKING.

WELL, MY EQUIPMENT IS READING A FOREIGN ENERGY SOURCE I'M NOT FAMILIAR WITH. ONE THAT SEEMS TO HAVE BONDED TO CLEO'S CELLS. AT FIRST I THOUGHT IT HAD SOMETHING TO DO WITH--I CAN'T BELIEVE I'M SAYING THIS--CONTACT WITH *ANCIENT TIME-TRAVELING TABLETS*, BUT NOW...

I'M NOT SO SURE.

WHATEVER IT IS, MY LATEST THEORY IS THAT THIS ENERGY GIVES YOU A BIT OF EXTRA ENDURANCE, WHICH IS WHY YOU CAN RUN FOR MILES ON END WITH LITTLE TO NO EFFORT, BUT IT NEEDS TO BE RELEASED EVERY SO OFTEN.

I DON'T THINK YOUR BODY IS MEANT TO CONTAIN IT.

AND THAT'S WHY SHE SUDDENLY ERUPTED LIKE A HOT-PINK VOLCANO?

FLATTERING.

WELL, YOU DID.

LIKE I SAID, IT'S JUST A THEORY.

I'M REALLY OUTSIDE MY WHEELHOUSE ON THIS ONE.

WHEN I WAS ON CADA'DUUN, ANTONY ALSO HAD A THEORY ABOUT THE GLOWING.

OH, **THIS** I GOTTA HEAR.

DON'T BE LIKE THAT, BRIAN. YOU HAVEN'T EVEN MET THE GUY.

ANTONY THOUGHT IT WAS A WARNING MECHANISM--A SORT OF...MAGIC MAKING ME AWARE OF POSSIBLE DANGER.

LIKE A KIND OF PROTECTION?

KINDA.

LOOK, I KNOW IT SOUNDS ODD, BUT I'M BARELY GLOWING ALL SUMMER, AND THEN...

FWOOSH! I ERUPT LIKE A...A HOT-PINK VOLCANO.

OKAY, I GUESS THAT IS A GOOD ANALOGY, AKILA.

THANK YOU.

I ERUPT LIKE A HOT-PINK VOLCANO RIGHT WHEN KHEPRA IS MENTIONING A POSSIBLE ATTACK ON CADA'DUUN. WHAT IF CADA'DUUN REALLY *IS* IN DANGER?

WHAT IF OCTAVIAN IS GOING BACK FOR THE *GOLDEN LION*?

IT DOES SEEM LIKE A WEIRD COINCIDENCE.

OCTAVIAN IS DEAD. HIS FLEET BLEW UP.

YOU DIDN'T SEE WHAT WE ALL DID ON HYKOSIS, BRIAN. HE HAD THE SWORD OF KEBECHET. A CAVE FELL ON HIM AND HE SNAPPED HIMSELF BACK TOGETHER LIKE HE WAS SIMPLY GETTING OUT OF BED IN THE MORNING.

A CAVE-IN AND AN EXPLOSION IN OUTER SPACE ARE TWO VERY DIFFERENT THINGS.

THERE'S... SOMETHING ELSE.

ON CADA'DUUN...

I...

WELL, I DIED.

YOU *WHAT?*

I...DIED. I WAS FIGHTING THIS BOUNTY HUNTER WHO WAS TRYING TO DESTROY THE GOLDEN LION.

ALTHOUGH NOW I THINK HE WAS WORKING FOR OCTAVIAN.

HE WAS BETTER THAN ME. HE IMPALED ME.

RIGHT HERE.

IT WAS DARK FOR A WHILE. COLD. BUT...I WOKE UP. FULLY HEALED.

I WAS GLOWING WHEN IT HAPPENED.

I'M SORRY, KHENSU. I SHOULD HAVE TOLD YOU BACK ON CADA'DUUN. WE SAID NO MORE LIES, BUT YOU GAVE ME THAT SINCERE APOLOGY ON HOW MUCH FAITH YOU HAD IN ME.

I DIDN'T KNOW HOW TO TELL YOU.

ARE YOU SURE YOU, UM...DIED? MAYBE YOU WERE JUST UNCON--

I'M SURE.

IT'S NOT A FEELING YOU FORGET.

MORE A LACK OF FEELING, REALLY.

MY POINT IS, I THINK OCTAVIAN AND I HAVE MORE IN COMMON THAN JUST A SHARED PAST. IF HE WERE REALLY DEAD, I'D KNOW IT.

HE'S NOT DEAD.

ALL THE MORE REASON TO GET THE SHIELD UP AND RUNNING.

WILL IT WORK?

WE'LL FIND OUT TONIGHT.

TONIGHT?

I THOUGHT THE LAUNCH WAS **TOMORROW!**

CLEO, YOU PASSED OUT. YOU'VE BEEN ASLEEP FOR, LIKE, TWENTY-EIGHT HOURS.

gah.

I HATE PASSING OUT.

HERE. MIHOS IS GOING TO KEEP YOU COMPANY WHILE KHENSU AND I HELP BRIAN.

MIHOS, DON'T LET CLEO DO ANYTHING STUPID LIKE LEAVE THAT BED.

CHIRP!

SORRY, CLEO. YOU KINDA HATE PARTIES ANYWAY, RIGHT?

I LIKE PARTIES WITH EXPLOSIONS.

THERE WON'T BE ANY EXPLOSIONS, CLEO.

ARE YOU KIDDING ME? THIS IS BRIAN'S PROJECT.

OF *COURSE* THERE WILL BE EXPLOSIONS!

GET SOME REST, CLEO. WE'LL TALK MORE ABOUT THIS IN THE MORNING.

TRY NOT TO BE GRUMPY.

CHIRP!

WELL, NOW WHAT? LOOKS LIKE WE MISSED OUR OPPORTUNITY TO BE PART OF THAT TEAM GOING TO CADA'DUUN.

WANT TO SKIP SCHOOL IN ORDER TO HELP SAVE A CIVILIZATION AND POSSIBLY THE ENTIRE GALAXY?

CHIRP.

YEAH, I GUESS THAT DIDN'T WORK OUT TOO WELL THE LAST TIME.

GUESS WE'LL JUST...SIT... HERE.

YAWN.

ACK! THIS IS SO **BORING.**

AND WHY HAVE I NOT SEEN A SINGLE DOCTOR SINCE I'VE WOKEN UP? THIS IS THE WORST INFIRMARY EVER.

C'MON, MIHOS, WE ARE GOING TO THAT SHIELD CELEBRATION.

CHIRP.

PLUK

I DON'T CARE WHAT AKILA SAID. I FEEL FINE.

CHIRP!

I BET THEY'LL HAVE LOTS OF **FOOOOOD** THERE...

CHIRP?

OH YEAH. TONS OF IT. POPCORN, CHOCOLATES, ICE CREAM, FRUIT BARS...

HEY!

WAIT UP!

HELLO.

DO YOU EVEN KNOW WHERE YOU'RE GO--

--OOOH.

PHARAOH YOSIRA.

CAT COUNCIL.

IT'S JUST "COUNCIL," CLEOPATRA.

OH. RIGHT.

HOW ARE YOU FEELING, CLEOPATRA? AFTER YESTERDAY, I ASSUMED YOU'D STILL BE ASSIGNED TO THE INFIRMARY.

NOTHING TO WORRY ABOUT, YOUR MAJESTY. FEELING BETTER THAN EVER, IN FACT.

ARE YOU SURE ABOUT THAT, CLEOPATRA?

HUH?

SEE? NEVER BETTER. HEH HEH.

EXCUSE ME, ADMINISTRANT, BUT WOULD YOU MIND IF I HAD A PRIVATE TALK WITH COUNCILOR TALIBATH?

IT'S ALL RIGHT. WHY DON'T THE REST OF YOU WALK ON AHEAD. I'LL MEET YOU AT THE LAUNCH.

VERY WELL.

KEEP IT QUICK, CLEOPATRA.

COUNCILOR, THIS IS GOING TO SOUND WEIRD, BUT I THINK SOMETHING MAY GO WRONG AT THE LAUNCH.

CLEOPATRA, BRIAN AND I HAVE GONE OVER EVERY DETAIL. EVERYTHING CHECKS OUT. TRUST ME, THE LAUNCH WILL BE *FINE*.

IT'S NOT THAT. IT'S JUST...MY GLOWING. SOMETIMES IT CAN ACT AS A SORT OF WARNING. OR, AT LEAST, I THINK IT DOES.

YESTERDAY IT HAPPENED WHILE ADMINISTRANT KHEPRA WAS TALKING ABOUT THE LAUNCH. NOW THAT IT'S IN LESS THAN AN HOUR, I'M GLOWING AGAIN.

I KNOW. IT SOUNDS CRAZY...

IT DOES, BUT SAFETY IS PARAMOUNT. I'LL HEAD BACK TO THE POWER CENTER AND GIVE THE SYSTEM ONE LAST INSPECTION. IF I NOTICE THE SLIGHTEST ANOMALY, I'LL SUSPEND THE LAUNCH.

NO, IT'S ALL RIGHT. CATCH UP TO THE OTHERS. LET THEM KNOW I'LL BE A LITTLE LATE TO THE CELEBRATION.

WILL DO!

THANKS, COUNCILOR.

REALLY? I MEAN, **GREAT!**

I'LL GO WITH YOU.

WERE YOU **STUDYING**?

NEVER MIND THAT.

WHAT ARE YOU DOING HERE? YOU'RE SUPPOSED TO BE RESTING!

WE'LL TALK ABOUT THIS LATER.

CHIRP

SOMETHING HAPPENED. WHERE'S BRIAN?

IN THE CONTROL ROOM.

WHAT DO YOU MEAN, SOMETHING HAPPENED?

I WAS GLOWING AGAIN.

AGAIN?

IT'S STARTING!

WHA?

VRRRUUMM

HUH?

CHIRP!

CLEO?

THERE SHE IS!

SORRY, CLEOPATRA. YOU'RE TO COME WITH US.

WHAT'S WRONG?

WHAT HAPPENED?

ALL OTHER CADETS ARE TO REPORT BACK TO THEIR DORMS.

ADMINISTRANT. WE HAVE HER.

I'M GOING WITH CLEO!

CHIRP!

IT'S ALL RIGHT, AKILA. YOU AND MIHOS MEET ME BACK IN OUR ROOM.

HERE SHE IS,
ADMINISTRANT.

TALIBATH?

WHAT'S GOING ON?

I WAS JUST ABOUT TO ASK YOUR CHARGE THE SAME THING.

COUNCILOR TALIBATH WAS LAST SEEN WITH YOU. WHAT DID YOU TWO TALK ABOUT?

OH NO. TALIBATH...

WE...I...TOLD HIM I THOUGHT THERE MIGHT BE A PROBLEM WITH THE SHIELD LAUNCH.

PROBLEM WITH THE LAUNCH? WHY DID YOU THINK THAT?

I WAS GLOWING. I THOUGHT MAYBE...

MAYBE SOMETHING BAD WOULD HAPPEN.

WELL, IT LOOKS LIKE YOU WERE CORRECT, CLEOPATRA.

ADMINISTRANT...

COUGH

COUGH

GET ON!

VWIIIISH

SECURITY SHIPS AFTER US.

I KNOW. DON'T YOU STILL HAVE A CHEETAH CELL INSTALLED ON THIS THING?

CHIRP!

VVRUM

OH YEAH!

BLIP

BLIP

BLIP

CHAPTER TWO

YOU SURE THIS IS THE RIGHT PLACE?

THAT'S WHAT BRIAN'S MESSAGE SAID.

HERE.

RUMMAGE
RUMMAGE

FOUND IT!

STEP STEP

NOW WHAT?

DUNNO.

BRIAN SAID TO JUST STAND ON THIS THING AND HE'LL--

FRAAAZK

FIND US.

WOW, THAT WORKED.

BRIAN!

CHIRP

HOLD ON. WHAT DO YOU MEAN, "THAT WORKED"?

WELL, THERE WAS THE *SLIIIIGHTEST* POSSIBILITY YOU WOULDN'T FULLY MATERIALIZE.

WHAT.

I THINK I'M GONNA BE SICK.

YEAH, I STILL HAVE SOME WORK TO DO ON IT. UNTIL TODAY, I ONLY TESTED IT ON FRUIT AND STUFF.

OH, SPEAKING OF WHICH...

I BROUGHT YOU SOME FOOD.

WHIIISH

NOM NOM

YOU GAVE IT **STEALTH** CAPABILITIES??

WELL, I COULDN'T EXACTLY BE SEEN WITH IT, COULD I?

ACK! THIS IS **RIDICULOUS**!

CLEO ISN'T A KILLER.

WE DON'T KNOW THAT, AKILA. WE STILL HAVE NO IDEA WHAT THIS ENERGY INSIDE OF ME IS.

BRIAN DOESN'T EVEN KNOW.

AND I **WAS** THE LAST PERSON TO SEE TALIBATH ALIVE.

STOP TALKING CRAZY, CLEO.

AKILA'S RIGHT. BYRON GOT BLASTED WITH A DIRECT OUTPOUR OF THAT ENERGY AND HE'S FINE.

MAYBE IT AFFECTS CATS DIFFERENTLY?

DOUBTFUL. OTHERWISE EVERY OTHER CAT YOU'VE COME INTO CONTACT WITH WOULD ALSO BE...

SO WHAT'S THE PLAN? WE CAN'T HIDE OUT **HERE** FOREVER.

HOW DO WE CONVINCE EVERYONE THAT CLEO IS INNOCENT SO WE CAN GO HOME?

THANKFULLY THE CONVINCING PART WON'T BE DIFFICULT. CLEO IS STILL TOO POPULAR A FIGURE FOR MOST PEOPLE TO BELIEVE SHE'S A TRAITOR. BUT UNFORTUNATELY ADMINISTRANT KHEPRA IS VERY INTENT ON BRINGING YOU IN.

BOTH OF YOU.

TRAITORS?

THAT'S WHAT SHE'S CLAIMING.

MAN, THIS IS TOTALLY GOING TO RUIN MY GPA.

HMM...

YOU'RE DOING IT AGAIN, BRIAN.

SORRY. I WAS THINKING ABOUT THE SHIELD.

CAN YOU FOCUS ON OUR CURRENT SITUATION FOR ONE MOMENT, BRIAN?

NO--I MEAN, **YES**, I AM. I WAS THINKING ABOUT THE KEY CODES.

munch munch

KEY CODES?

THE SHIELD WAS DESIGNED USING THERMODYNAMIC TECHNOLOGY. ESSENTIALLY, MAYET'S ATMOSPHERE IS WHAT WILL POWER THE GRID INDEFINITELY, SO EVEN IF THE CONTROL CENTER IS COMPROMISED, THE SHIELD WILL REMAIN FUNCTIONAL. IT WAS MEANT AS A SAFEGUARD AGAINST ATTACK.

THE ONLY WAY TO REALLY SHUT IT DOWN IS BY ENTERING A KEY CODE. BUT ONLY A SMALL NUMBER OF HIGH-RANKING INDIVIDUALS INSIDE P.Y.R.A.M.I.D. WERE GIVEN ACCESS TO ONE.

EVEN I DON'T HAVE ONE.

COUNCILOR TALIBATH WAS ONE OF THOSE INDIVIDUALS.

SO YOU THINK THERE REALLY *IS* A TRAITOR AT P.Y.R.A.M.I.D.? SOMEONE KILLED TALIBATH FOR HIS KEY CODE?

OR SOMEONE KILLED TALIBATH SO THEY WERE THE ONLY ONE WHO HAD IT.

DO YOU KNOW WHO ELSE HAD ONE?

OKAY, SHE CAN BE KIND OF INTENSE--AND SURE, SHE HAS SEEMED TO HAVE HAD IT IN FOR CLEO SINCE SHE GOT HERE-- BUT KHEPRA'S DONE MORE TO HELP THE NILE GALAXY THAN ANYONE.

SHE CERTAINLY WOULDN'T **MURDER** SOMEONE.

HMM...

OH, GREAT. NOW YOU'RE DOING IT.

THE ADMINISTRANT DOESN'T HOLD THE HIGHEST RANK.

THE PHARAOH DOES.

HEY--YOU'RE RIGHT!

PHARAOH YOSIRA IS RANKED ABOVE EVERYONE.

YOU BOTH AREN'T SERIOUSLY IMPLYING THAT PHARAOH YOSIRA IS THE TRAITOR?

OF COURSE NOT. BUT IF SHE HAS A KEY CODE, AND SOMEONE IS GOING AROUND MURDERING THOSE WHO HAVE ONE...

BUT PHARAOH YOSIRA HASN'T TAKEN AN ACTIVE ROLE AT P.Y.R.A.M.I.D. IN ALL THE TIME I'VE BEEN HERE. SHE SEEMS MORE THAN COMFORTABLE LETTING THE COUNCIL HANDLE EVERYTHING.

THERE'S NO WAY SHE HAS A KEY CODE.

IT DOESN'T MATTER.

WE NEED TO WARN HER. EVEN IF SOMEONE **THINKS** SHE HAS ONE...

OKAY. BUT HOW? IT'S NOT LIKE WE CAN JUST WALK INTO PHARAOH YOSIRA'S ROOM AND TELL HER OUR SUSPICIONS.

WHY NOT?

UM, BECAUSE WE'RE FUGITIVES. AND SHE'S THE **PHARAOH**.

BUT IF NO ONE SEES US...

OKAY, LISTEN UP.

I HAVE A PLAN...

TELL ME AGAIN WHY WE DECIDED TO FOLLOW CLEO'S PLAN?

I'M TRYING TO FIGURE THAT OUT MYSELF.

C'MON, GUYS. IT'S A GOOD PLAN!

THE PLAN!

WELL?

CHIRP.

Sigh.

OKAY, I'LL EXPLAIN IT.

BRIAN USES HIS NOT-YET-A-FUGITIVE SELF TO GAIN ACCESS TO THE MAIN ENTRANCE OF GRIFFIN TOWER.

WHAT DO YOU MEAN, "NOT *YET* A FUGITIVE"?

AND WHY THE MAIN ENTRANCE? PHARAOH YOSIRA'S LIVING QUARTERS ARE ON THE TOP FLOOR.

GUYS, I'M GETTING THERE. PAY ATTENTION.

ONCE INSIDE, BRIAN FINDS A SECURE ROOM FOR ONE OF HIS CRAZY TRANSPORT MAT THINGIES THAT HE'S BEEN ABLE TO SNEAK IN WITH HIM.

WHAT? NO WAY.

I AM NOT GETTING ON ONE OF THOSE THINGS AGAIN.

YOU WON'T HAVE TO.

WHILE I'M GETTING TRANSPORTED *INTO* THE BUILDING...

YOU'RE ON THE *OUTSIDE* OF IT USING MY NOW STEALTH-ENHANCED BIKE--THANKS, BRIAN--TO LAND ON THE ROOF OF THE TOWER.

BUT I CAN ONLY GAIN ACCESS TO SO MANY FLOORS. HOW ARE YOU GOING TO GET TO THE TOP LEVEL? NOT TO MENTION AVOID ANY SECURITY?

SIMPLE...

THE AIR DUCTS.

YOU'RE GOING TO CRAWL UP THE AIR DUCTS.

WHY NOT?

HOW ARE YOU GOING TO KNOW WHERE YOU'RE GOING?

THAT'S WHY YOU'RE GOING TO STAY IN THAT SECURE ROOM YOU FOUND TO GUIDE ME THROUGH THEM USING A MAP OF THE VENTILATION SYSTEM.

＊

ACTUALLY, THAT'S NOT A BAD PLAN.

HELLO?

I'M STILL ON THE ROOF.

OH YEAH. YOU'RE GOING TO NEED A CABLE AND A HARNESS.

WITH THE CABLE SECURED TO THE ROOF, YOU'RE GOING TO CLIMB DOWN TO YOSIRA'S WINDOW...

USE SUCTION CUPS TO ATTACH TO THE WALL...

AND INFORM ME WHEN IT'S SAFE TO ENTER HER ROOM.

ALL CLEAR!

WHY CAN'T I JUST HOVER IN FRONT OF HER WINDOW IN STEALTH MODE?

WELL, SURE. IF YOU WANT TO DO IT THE EASY WAY.

YES, CLEO! I WANT TO DO THIS THE EASY WAY!

FINE. SO WHILE AKILA IS HOVERING IN FRONT OF YOSIRA'S WINDOW...

WHICH DOES NOT SOUND CREEPY AT ALL.

I WILL DROP INTO HER ROOM--COMPLETELY UNDETECTED--EXPLAIN THE SITUATION, AND THE THREE OF US WILL USE MY BIKE TO TAKE HER BACK TO BRIAN'S CREEPY OLD FACTORY HOME.

SO NOW WE ARE ADDING KIDNAPPING THE PHARAOH TO OUR LABEL OF TRAITOROUS COUNCILOR KILLERS?

ASSUMED TRAITOROUS COUNCILOR KILLERS, AKILA.

ASSUMED.

IS THIS REALLY THE BEST PLAN?

DO YOU HAVE A BETTER ONE?

CLANG
CLANG

OH! YOSIRA JUST ENTERED HER ROOM.

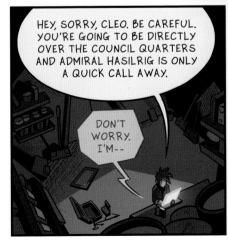

SHE'S ALONE!

I CAN'T BELIEVE THIS MIGHT ACTUALLY WORK.

WHAT DO YOU MEAN YOU CAN'T BELIE--

HEY, SORRY, CLEO. BE CAREFUL. YOU'RE GOING TO BE DIRECTLY OVER THE COUNCIL QUARTERS AND ADMIRAL HASILRIG IS ONLY A QUICK CALL AWAY.

DON'T WORRY. I'M--

CLEO?

105

GRANDFATHER...

CLANG

HI, YOUR MAJESTY.

PLEASE BACK AWAY FROM THE WINDOW.

DROP

VRRUM

VZZZSH

ADMINISTRANT.

WHAT IS IT?

CLEOPATRA HAS BEEN SPOTTED IN THE TOWER. SHE'S ON THE PHARAOH'S FLOOR.

ALERT THE PHARAOH'S PERSONAL GUARDS.

WE HAVE, MA'AM...

THEY AREN'T RESPONDING.

GOOD-BYE, VALEDICTORIAN HONORS.

ARE...ARE YOU SURE?

PLEASE, I NEED YOU TO DO THIS, YOUR MAJESTY. YOU'RE THE ONLY PERSON I CAN TRUST.

I DON'T...

LISTEN, I UNDERSTAND THE PRESSURES OF BEING PHARAOH. MAYBE MORE THAN ANYONE. BACK IN EGYPT, I NEVER WANTED THE BURDENS OF BEING A QUEEN, NOT TO MENTION ONE WHO IS RESPONSIBLE FOR AN ENTIRE GALAXY.

BUT I'VE COME TO REALIZE IT'S NOT ABOUT ME. BEING A SAVIOR. RULING A KINGDOM. THOSE THINGS DON'T MAKE US MORE IMPORTANT THAN THE PEOPLE WE ARE ENTRUSTED TO PROTECT. IT'S THE OPPOSITE OF THAT.

AND YOUR PEOPLE NEED YOU.

OWWWWW.

HUH.

IT WORKED.

CLEO!

KHENSU!

AKILA!

ARE YOU ALL RIGHT?

ARE *YOU* ALL RIGHT? AKILA'S BEEN FILLING ME IN, BUT SAYS THIS WASN'T PART OF THE ORIGINAL PLAN.

GETTING OURSELVES ARRESTED CERTAINLY DOES CRY OUT AS A LITTLE CRAZY, CLEO.

CONGRATULATIONS, CLEOPATRA...

I'VE BEEN SPENDING MONTHS TRYING TO CONVINCE THE COUNCIL NOT TO SEND YOU BACK TO YOUR OWN TIME, BUT YOU'VE UNRAVELED ALL THAT EFFORT IN LESS THAN A WEEK.

HAVE I?

HAVE I, KHEPRA?

UM. YES. YOU HAVE.

HAAAAAAAVE I?

...PRACTICALLY HANDED HER TO YOU ON A SILVER PLATTER AND SHE EVADED YOU BOTH TIMES. NOW I'VE BEEN TASKED WITH WHAT *YOU* FAILED TO DO.

CAREFUL TO MIND YOUR TONE, KHEPRA. IT APPEARS THAT SHE'S EVADED YOU AS WELL.

IT'S ONLY A MATTER OF TIME BEFORE CLEOPATRA IS LOCATED. JUST BE SURE YOU KEEP TO YOUR END OF OUR BARGAIN, OCTAVIAN.

AFTER WHAT HAPPENED WITH CADA'DUUN, KHEPRA?

FOR YOUR SAKE, YOU HAD BETTER ABIDE BY YOURS.

VZZSH

C'MONNN...

C'MON...

WHERE ARE YOU?

AH!

?

SHIFF

126

VRRRR

TELL THE ENGINEERS TO GET TO WORK AND CONTINUE COURSE FOR MAYET.

IT IS TIME WE FINALLY PUT AN END TO P.Y.R.A.M.I.D.

CHAPTER THREE

FIVE
HOURS
AGO

THE TROUBLING REVELATION OF KHEPRA'S COMMUNICATION WITH OCTAVIAN HAS LED TO FURTHER DISCONCERTING NEWS.

THROUGH OUR INTERROGATION, WE'VE LEARNED THAT OUR NEW ALLIES IN CADA'DUUN WERE INDEED SUBJECT TO AN ATTACK. WHAT WE THOUGHT TO BE A ROGUE XERX VESSEL IN THE ELTORIAN SYSTEM WAS NOTHING BUT A DECOY.

OCTAVIAN, WHO WE NOW KNOW TO BE VERY MUCH ALIVE, AMBUSHED OUR REINFORCEMENTS AND HAS OCCUPIED THE CADA'DUUNIAN CITY.

OCCUPIED?!

COUNCILOR--SORRY-- **ADMINISTRANT** KEK. BUT HAVE ANY... I MEAN...

I'M AFRAID WE'VE HAD NO COMMUNICATION WITH ANY OF THE PLANET'S POPULACE, ALTHOUGH RECOVERED TRANSMISSIONS SUGGEST A FEW SHIPS MIGHT HAVE BEEN ABLE TO ESCAPE BEFORE THE ATTACK.

I'M SORRY, CADET THEORIS. THAT'S ALL WE KNOW.

THERE'S STILL A CHANCE YOUR PARENTS ARE SAFE.

IT GETS WORSE.

WE RECENTLY RECEIVED A DISTRESS BEACON FROM THE REMOTE PLANET OF HYKOSIS. WHEN OUR CLOSEST SHIPS WENT TO INVESTIGATE, THEY DISCOVERED THE PLANET'S ONLY CITY WAS NO LONGER THERE.

YOU ARE ASKING US TO PUT THE LIVES OF EVERY PLANET THAT'S PART OF THIS SYSTEM IN JEOPARDY BASED ON A FEELING YOU CAN'T EXPLAIN?

I'M SORRY, BUT I WON'T--

I TRUST HER.

I DO, TOO.

ME TOO!

I TRUST HER AS WELL.

AGREED.

YES, LET THE SAVIOR SAVE US.

THAT'S WHY SHE'S HERE.

SHE'S PROVEN HERSELF!

WE BELIEVE IN HER!

WELL, CLEOPATRA...

IT LOOKS LIKE YOU MAY JUST GET YOUR WISH.

HASILRIG?

VERY WELL. OUR FLEET WILL KEEP OCTAVIAN ENGAGED WHILE CLEO--

AND KHENSU!

I'LL NEED A COPILOT.

nod

--WHILE CLEOPATRA AND KHENSU INFILTRATE THE XERX ENGINEERING SHIP.

YOU WERE ELECTED TO PROTECT THIS SYSTEM, NOT BETRAY IT!

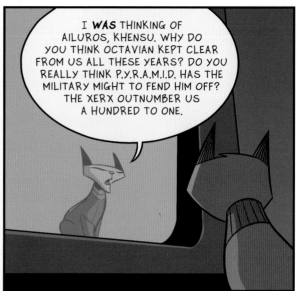

I **WAS** THINKING OF AILUROS, KHENSU. WHY DO YOU THINK OCTAVIAN KEPT CLEAR FROM US ALL THESE YEARS? DO YOU REALLY THINK P.Y.R.A.M.I.D. HAS THE MILITARY MIGHT TO FEND HIM OFF? THE XERX OUTNUMBER US A HUNDRED TO ONE.

WE HAVE CLEOPATRA.

DON'T BE NAÏVE.

I EXPECT HER TO SAVE US.

I STILL DO.

YOU SOUND LIKE YOUR FATHER.

THEN I SOUND LIKE SOMEONE WHO BELIEVES IN SOMETHING MORE THAN THEMSELF!

THAT KIND OF THINKING IS WHAT GOT HIM KILLED.

SHUFF

BAM

PZEW

PZEW

PZEW

BAM

ZAP

ZAP

PZEW

PZEW

BOOM

CAREFUL!

I WAS BEING CAREFUL! IT'S NOT EASY TO AVOID THESE CHROME TOPS WHEN THEY CAN'T SEE YOU.

THERE.

BETWEEN THOSE TWO WALLS.

THAT LOOKS LIKE A GOOD PLACE TO LAND.

YOU CHARGED YOUR RAY GUN, RIGHT?

OF COURSE I CHARGED IT. DO YOU EVEN NEED TO ASK?

OKAY, OKAY.

POINT TAKEN.

KHENSU...

IF--

DON'T SAY IT.

SAPPY DOESN'T SUIT YOU.

READY?

READY.

148

MAYET'S SHIELD IS STILL UP. YOUR WEAPON IS USELESS HERE.

HA.

I ASSUME YOU ARE REFERRING TO THAT COWARD OF A CAT, KHEPRA.

SHE SHOWED HER ALLEGIANCE WHEN SHE DECIDED NOT TO GIVE UP HER CODES AFTER MY ATTACK ON CADA'DUUN.

AN ATTACK SHE TRIED TO PREVENT.

NO, SORRY. I'M AFRAID THAT PRECIOUS SHIELD OF YOURS WILL BE QUITE INEFFECTIVE AT ANY MOMENT NOW.

INEFFECTIVE?

...

THERE'S ANOTHER SPY.

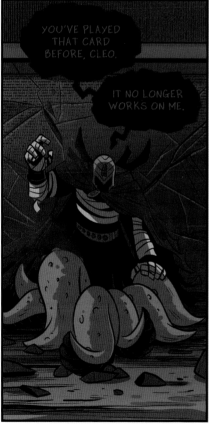

YOU'VE PLAYED THAT CARD BEFORE, CLEO.

IT NO LONGER WORKS ON ME.

FLASH

FWIISH

SSHH

WELL, THIS STINKS.

HASILRIG SAYS WE'RE HOLDING OUR OWN BUT WE'RE STILL VASTLY OUTNUMBERED.

A LOT IS RIDING ON CLEO RIGHT NOW.

I SHOULD BE UP THERE WITH HER.

BEEP
BEEP
BEEP

KHENSU!

VZZSH

AKILA?

AND BRIAN.

WHAT'S WRONG, KHENSU?

WHERE'S CLEO?

SHE'S... LOOK, YOU NEED TO WARN PHARAOH YOSIRA. I'M NOT SURE WHO ELSE YOU CAN TRUST.

THERE'S ANOTHER SPY IN P.Y.R.A.M.I.D.

ANOTHER ONE? WHAT DO YOU MEAN, ANOTHER ONE?

THE XERX KNEW WE WERE COMING. OCTAVIAN WAS PREPARED.

THE SHIELD MAY BE COMPROMISED.

IT'S OKAY. EVEN IF THERE IS ANOTHER SPY, ADMINISTRANT KHEPRA WAS THE ONLY ONE WITH THE KEY CODES AND SHE'S...

WHERE'S...

WHAT IS IT?

WITH KHEPRA LOCKED UP, HER SHIELD ACCESS WOULD HAVE TRANSFERRED TO THE NEXT HIGHEST RANKING P.Y.R.A.M.I.D. OFFICER.

NEXT HIGHEST...

BUT THAT WOULD BE...

C'MON!

AAH!!!

BLAZT

CRACK

UGH.

WHY ARE YOU DOING THIS, GOZI? HOW DID YOU BECOME SUCH A MONSTER?

A MONSTER?

ME?

YOU DID THIS TO ME, BY ABANDONING ME IN THAT TOMB.

TOMB? YOU MEAN BACK IN EGYPT?

ARE YOU SERIOUS? I DIDN'T LEAVE ON PURPOSE!

BUT YOU NEVER RETURNED.

DO YOU KNOW WHAT HAPPENED AFTER YOU LEFT, CLEO? DO YOU KNOW WHAT HAPPENED TO THE KINGDOM YOU NEVER WANTED?

I...I NEVER...?

IT WAS DESTROYED, BY NOTHING MORE THAN GREEDY SPACE PIRATES SAILING ACROSS THE UNIVERSE SEARCHING FOR TREASURE.

THEY BURNED IT TO THE GROUND. YOUR FAMILY. OUR PEOPLE. ALL OF IT.

AND I, IN TURN...

WAS LEFT LIKE THIS.

GOZI...

YOU COULD HAVE STOPPED IT. YOU CLEARLY HAD THE POWER IN YOU TO DO SO. BUT EVER SINCE I LEARNED OF THE PROPHECY...THAT YOU WERE DESTINED TO SAVE THIS WORLD, NOT OURS...AND THAT YOU CHOSE THEM OVER US...

I'VE NEVER.

STOPPED.

HATING YOU.

COUGH

COUGH

COUGH

I DIDN'T KNOW, GOZI.

I DIDN'T KNOW ABOUT EGYPT.

IF I DID...

YOU WOULD HAVE WHAT? LEFT THE PLACE YOU NOW CALL HOME? THE PLACE YOU ARE FATED TO PROTECT?

IF IT...

UGH...

MEANT SAVING... YOU.

IT DOESN'T MATTER.

YOUR PLASMA WEAPON IS NOTHING BUT MOLTEN ROCK NOW. P.Y.R.A.M.I.D. CAN STILL DEFEAT YOU.

OH, CLEO.

I DIDN'T THINK ONE SPY IN YOUR MIDST WAS SUFFICIENT.

DID YOU REALLY THINK I'D BE SO INCAUTIOUS AS TO ONLY INSTALL A SINGLE PLASMA WEAPON IN THIS FLEET?

CHAK CHAK CHAK CHAK

KLANG KLANG KLANG

VRRRRUMMMMMMBLE

THUM

BLIP BLIP BLIP BLIP

THE HOLDING CELLS.

THEY COLLAPSED.

IT'S OKAY. YOU DON'T HAVE TO--

BLIP

BLIP

BLIP BLIP BLIP

THE EVACUATION WAS SO SUDDEN THEY DIDN'T HAVE TIME TO TAKE ALL THE NECESSARY PRECAUTIONS.

I DIDN'T KILL TALIBATH, KHENSU. YOU NEED TO KNOW I WOULD NEVER...

I KNOW. IT WAS KEK. HE TRIED TO SABOTAGE THE LAUNCH. WE'VE DETAINED HIM.

MY CONCERN WAS ALWAYS FOR THE SAFETY OF AILUROS. THE AGREEMENT WAS CLEOPATRA IN EXCHANGE FOR OUR SECURITY.

I SHOULD HAVE KNOWN BETTER. I SHOULD HAVE...

I'M SORRY I LET YOU DOWN. I'M SORRY I DIDN'T TREAT YOU LIKE A SON.

MOM...

YOU REALLY ARE SO MUCH LIKE YOUR FATHER. HE WOULD HAVE BEEN PROUD TO SEE WHAT YOU'VE BECOME.

BRAVE.

BLIP   BLIP

I HOPE THAT CLEOPATRA FULFILLS THE DESTINY YOU SO DESPERATELY WANT TO BE TRUE. I...

BLI///

OH, YOU KNOW, THE USUAL. LIZARDS, RATS, SPIDERS...

YOU'VE HIT SPIDERS WITH THAT THING?

REALLY?

WATCH THIS.

STREEEETCH

TWANG

POK

POK

POK

POK

UM...THERE WAS A SPIDER RIGHT THERE.

HEH.

HA HA HA

HA HA HA HA HA HA HA HA HA HA HA HA

SPECIAL THANKS TO:

My beautiful, loving wife, Jen. Apologies for all the spoilers.

My two boys, Oliver and Orion. I promise to try to fit a dinosaur into the next book.

My cat, Misty, for the gentle purrs and company. The clawing at my leg while I'm working I could do without, but the purring has been aces.

The rest of my *super* supportive friends and family. I'm continually blessed to have so many of you in my life.

Cassandra Pelham Fulton and David Saylor for keeping this series steering in the right direction, Phil Falco for making it look so good, and all the other wonderful folks at Scholastic for the amazing work you've put into it. One more book to go!

My wonderful agent, Judy Hansen. I hope you like dinosaurs.

My incredible team of color flatters: Mary Bellamy, Kate Carleton, Lee Cherolis, Dan Conner, Josh Dykstra, Patricia Krmpotich, and Rachel Polk. I couldn't have gotten this book done on time (well, close to on time) without you.

Christ, for helping with the tough stuff. The easy stuff, too, I suppose.

And last but not least, the artists around the world crafting stories and music. I would be completely directionless if not for your inspiration and melodies.

EXTRA SPECIAL THANKS TO:

All the teachers, librarians, booksellers, parents, and readers out there who have supported Cleopatra in Space and/or given me high fives. CONTINUE TO BE AWESOME!

ABOUT THE AUTHOR

A graduate of the Columbus College of Art & Design, Mike Maihack spends his time drawing comics, writing comics, talking about comics, and whatever one does to ensure his house doesn't collapse from two boys bouncing around inside it (which sometimes involves comics). He's contributed to several books, including Sensation Comics Featuring Wonder Woman; *Parable*; Jim Henson's *The Storyteller*; *Cow Boy*; *Geeks, Girls, and Secret Identities*; and *Comic Book Tattoo*. The first book in the Cleopatra in Space series, *Target Practice*, was a Florida Book Award winner, a YALSA Great Graphic Novel for Teens, and a YALSA Quick Pick. Mike lives in Lutz, Florida, with his family.

The creation of *Fallen Empires* took seventeen months, sixteen of which were spent growing that beard in the above drawing. To learn more (about Mike, not growing a beard), visit him online at www.mikemaihack.com.

BOOK ONE
TARGET PRACTICE

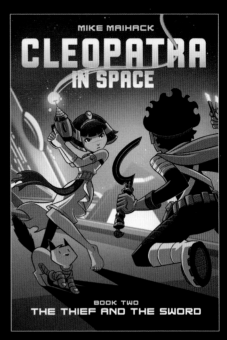

BOOK TWO
THE THIEF AND THE SWORD

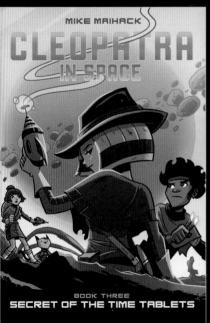

BOOK THREE
SECRET OF THE TIME TABLETS

BOOK FOUR
THE GOLDEN LION